MIDLOTHIAN
PUBLIC LIBRARY

DEMCO

Cindy, Cedric, and the Circus

MIDLOTHIAN PUBLIC LIBRARY
14701 S. KENTON AVE.
MIDLOTHIAN, IL 60445

The Sound of Soft C

by Cecilia Minden and Joanne Meier · illustrated by Bob Ostrom

Published by The Child's World®
1980 Lookout Drive
Mankato, MN 56003-1705
800-599-READ
www.childsworld.com

The Child's World®: Mary Berendes, Publishing Director
The Design Lab: Design and page production

Copyright © 2011 by The Child's World®
All rights reserved. No part of this book may be reproduced or utilized in any form or by any means without written permission from the publisher.

Library of Congress Cataloging-in-Publication Data
Minden, Cecilia.
Cindy, Cedric and the circus : the sound of soft c / by Cecilia Minden and Joanne Meier ; illustrated by Bob Ostrom.
p. cm.
ISBN 978-1-60253-396-7 (library bound : alk. paper)
1. English language–Consonants–Juvenile literature. 2. English language–Phonetics–Juvenile literature 3. Reading–Phonetic method–Juvenile literature. I. Title.
PE1159.M563 2010
[E]–dc22 2010002908

Printed in the United States of America in Mankato, MN.
July 2010
F11538

NOTE TO PARENTS AND EDUCATORS:

The Child's World® has created this series with the goal of exposing children to engaging stories and illustrations that assist in phonics development. The books in the series will help children learn the relationships between the letters of written language and the individual sounds of spoken language. This contact helps children learn to use these relationships to read and write words.

The books in this series follow a similar format. An introductory page, to be read by an adult, introduces the child to the phonics feature, or sound, that will be highlighted in the book. Read this page to the child, stressing the phonic feature. Help the student learn how to form the sound with her mouth. The story and engaging illustrations follow the introduction. At the end of the story, word lists categorize the feature words into their phonic elements.

Each book in this series has been carefully written to meet specific readability requirements. Close attention has been paid to elements such as word count, sentence length, and vocabulary. Readability formulas measure the ease with which the text can be read and understood. Each book in this series has been analyzed using the Spache readability formula.

Reading research suggests that systematic phonics instruction can greatly improve students' word recognition, spelling, and comprehension skills. This series assists in the teaching of phonics by providing students with important opportunities to apply their knowledge of phonics as they read words, sentences, and text.

The letter c makes two sounds.

The hard sound of **c** sounds like **c** as in: *cap* and *coat.*

The soft sound of **c** sounds like **c** as in: *celery* and *centipede.*

In this book, you will read words that have the soft **c** sound as in: *circus, city, cents,* and *circle.*

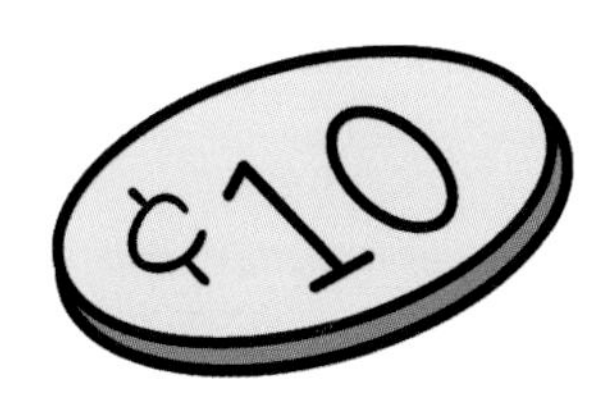

Cindy and Cedric are excited.

They are going to the circus.

The circus is in the city.

BUS
STOP

A bus will take them to the city. They wait and wait.

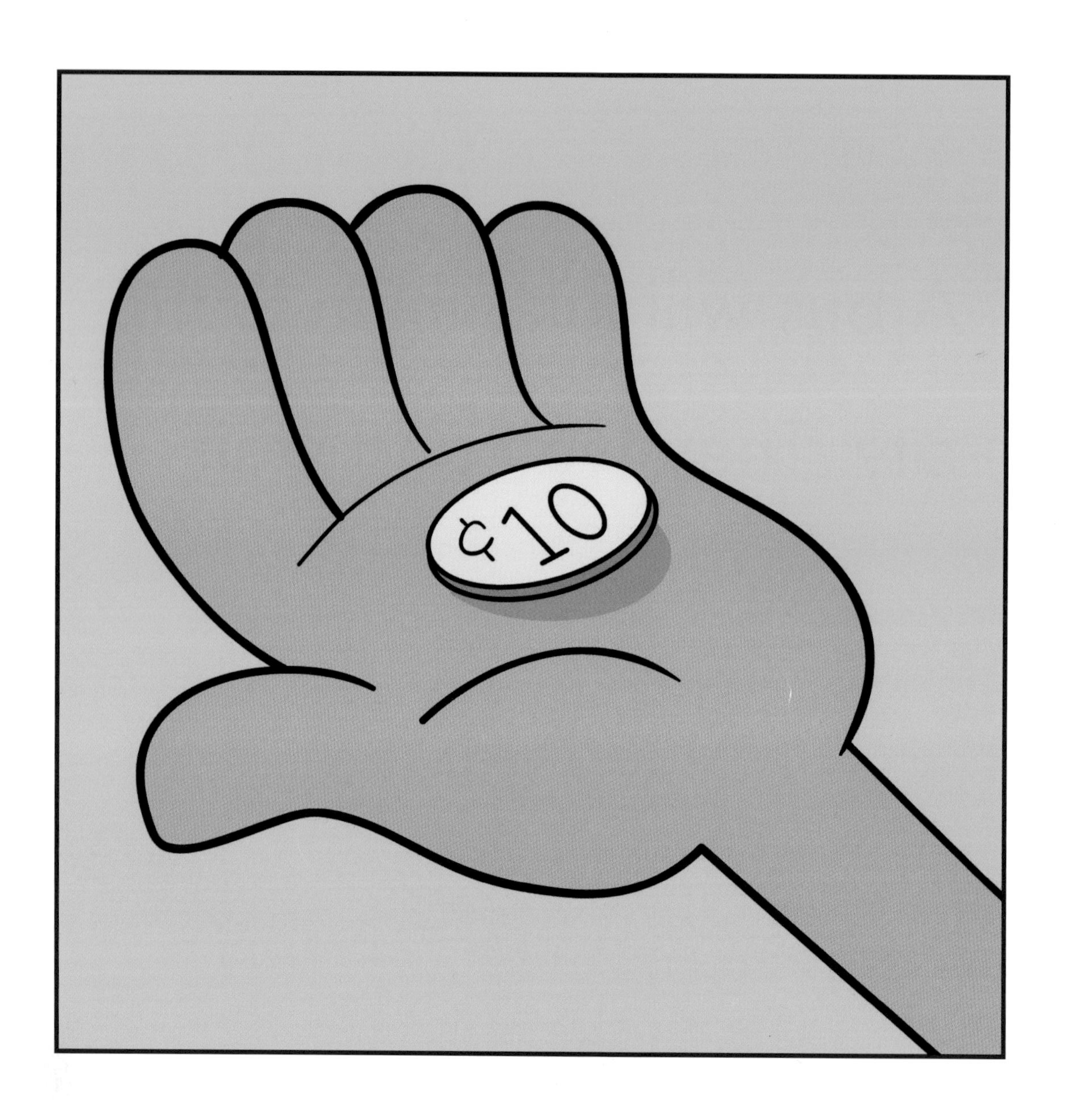
¢10

Here comes the bus. It is ten cents to ride the bus.

CIRCUS

The bus ride is fun!

Soon they are at the circus.

Celine the clown is in the center ring. She makes Cindy and Cedric laugh!

Here come the tigers. They run fast around the circle.

Look at the monkey.

He is riding a bicycle.

Are you having fun?

We are certain we are!

Fun Facts

Early bicycles were called by several different names, including walking machines, bone shakers, and hobby horses. In the late 1800s, bicycle races became popular in the United States. Some of these races involved riders traveling nonstop for six days at a time! The winner was whomever could travel the farthest during this period.

Mumbai, India, is the largest individual city in the world and has more than 12 million residents. New York City is the largest individual city within the United States and has more than 8 million people. Scientists believe the first ancient cities appeared about 5,500 years ago.

Activity

A Bicycle Trip with Your Family

If you like bike riding, plan a bicycle trip with your family. Pick an area that has several good bike trails. Discuss what equipment you will need. Pack plenty of bottled water, sunscreen, a healthy snack, and helmets. Take breaks every so often so you don't get too tired. Also, remember to be safe and to look out for other riders who share the trail with you.

To Learn More

Books

About the Sound of Soft C

Moncure, Jane Belk. *My "c" Sound Box®*. Mankato, MN: The Child's World, 2009.

About Bicycles

Best, Cari, and Christine Davenier (illustrator). *Sally Jean, the Bicycle Queen*. New York: Farrar, Straus and Giroux, 2006.

Gibbons, Gail. *Bicycle Book*. New York: Holiday House, 1995.

About Circuses

Millman, Isaac. *Moses Goes to the Circus*. New York: Frances Foster Books, 2003.

Spier, Peter. *Peter Spier's Circus!* New York: Bantam Doubleday Dell Books for Young Readers, 1995.

About Cities

Harris, Nicholas. *A Day in a City*. Minneapolis, MN: Millbrook Press, 2004.

Neubecker, Robert. *Wow! City!* New York: Hyperion Books for Children, 2004.

Web Sites

Visit our home page for lots of links about the Sound of Soft C:

childsworld.com/links

Note to Parents, Teachers, and Librarians: We routinely check our Web links to make sure they're safe, active sites—so encourage your readers to check them out!

Soft C Feature Words

Proper Names

Cedric
Celine
Cindy

Feature Words in Initial Position

center
cents
certain
circle
circus
city

Feature Words in Medial Position

bicycle
excited

About the Authors

Cecilia Minden, PhD, is the former director of the Language and Literacy Program at the Harvard Graduate School of Education. She is now a reading consultant for school and library publications. She earned her PhD in reading education from the University of Virginia. Cecilia and her husband, Dave Cupp, live outside Chapel Hill, North Carolina. They enjoy sharing their love of reading with their grandchildren, Chelsea and Qadir.

Joanne Meier, PhD, has worked as an elementary school teacher, university professor, and researcher. She earned her BA in early childhood education from the University of South Carolina, and her MEd and PhD in education from the University of Virginia. She currently works as a literacy consultant for schools and private organizations. Joanne lives in Virginia with her husband Eric, daughters Kella and Erin, two cats, and a gerbil.

About the Illustrator

Bob Ostrom has been illustrating children's books for nearly twenty years. A graduate of the New England School of Art & Design at Suffolk University, Bob has worked for such companies as Disney, Nickelodeon, and Cartoon Network. He lives in North Carolina with his wife Melissa and three children, Will, Charlie, and Mae.